THE HAUNTED GARGOYLE

Look for these books in the
Clue™ series:

THE HAUNTED GARGOYLE

Book created by **A. E. Parker**

Written by **Marie Jacks**

Based on characters from the Parker Brothers® game

A Creative Media Applications Production

SCHOLASTIC INC.
New York Toronto London Auckland Sydney

Special thanks to: Susan Nash, Laura Millhollin, Maureen Taxter, Jean Feiwel, Ellie Berger, Greg Holch, Dona Smith, Nancy Smith, John Simko, Karen Hudson, David Tommasino, and Elizabeth Parisi

ISBN 0-590-62375-3

Copyright © 1995 by Waddingtons Games, a division of Hasbro UK Limited. All rights reserved. Published by Scholastic Inc. by arrangement with Parker Brothers, a division of Tonka Corporation. CLUE® is a registered trademark of Waddingtons Games Ltd. for its detective game equipment.

12 11 10 9 8 7 6 5 4 3 2 1   5 6 7 8 9/9 0/0

Printed in the U.S.A.   40

First Scholastic printing, March 1996

To Dee Paddock, Dan Hubbard,
De Hubbard, and Bud Hubbard

Contents

THE HAUNTED GARGOYLE

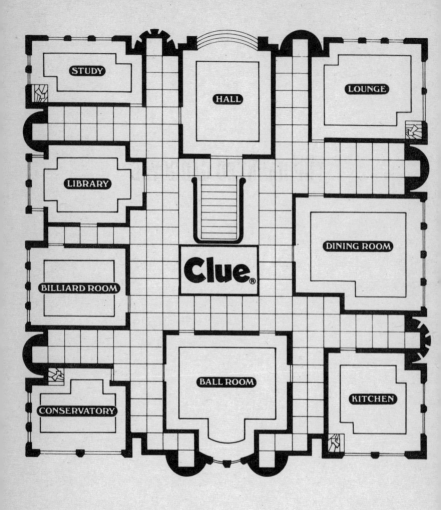

Allow Me to Introduce Myself . . .

GREETINGS! MY NAME IS REGINALD Boddy — but you can call me Mr. Boddy. Please don't be offended. I happen to prefer Mister to Reginald, that's all.

To those of you who have a *clue* as to what happens here at my mansion, I say, "Welcome back!"

To newcomers, all I can say is, "Sharpen your pencils and your crime-solving skills."

I certainly could have used your help last time, when I was murdered over a life insurance policy. Imagine a bunch of normally wonderful friends committing a murder over a piece of paper! Granted, the policy was worth three million dollars, but should a few million dollars come between friends?

Oh, don't worry. I feared my friends might try something, so I replaced the real Knife with a trick one with a retractable blade. I ended up fooling the would-be murderer. And the insurance policy? It's safely tucked inside my safe, where it shall stay safe for a long, long time.

If a test of friendship is the ability to forgive another person's mistakes, then I've certainly been tested. In fact, to show there are no hard feelings, I've invited my friends back for another visit to my mansion.

In a few moments I shall be joining them in the Ball Room. May I beg your assistance in helping me keep track of them? If you help me, I will consider *you* a true-blue friend.

There are six friends (or guests, as we refer to all visitors at the mansion) including my loyal, if sometimes moldy — I mean, moody — maid, Mrs. White. (I will never be a suspect in any wrongdoing. You have my word, as a gentleman.)

The six guests you need to keep track of are:

Mr. Green: He'll do anything to make a buck. I heard he even cheated his own grandmother in a business deal. How do I know this rumor is true? Because Green's grandmother told me herself!

Colonel Mustard: A gentleman who remembers the days when men were men, and real men loved duels. Be careful not to have a cross word with him, or you may find yourself crossing swords.

Mrs. Peacock: A refined lady who understands that a society is measured by how well it adheres to proper manners. She lives by this rule, except on the occasion when I find her fingers adhering to one of my valuables.

2

Professor Plum: A wonderful, if somewhat forgetful, companion. I ask you, how many people have the ability to forget the names of their parents, their own birthdays, and hometowns? Plum claims he remembers what's really important, though he can't seem to remember what that is.

Miss Scarlet: The woman understands that appearances are often deceiving. She uses her world-famous beauty and refined sense of fashion to deceive many an unsuspecting person. When you label her a *femme fatale*, she takes it as a compliment.

Mrs. White: As my loyal maid for these many years, she keeps track of the various comings and goings at the mansion. In fact, she has participated in more than a few of the "goings" of my possessions. Still, good help is hard to find nowadays. And, believe me, the poor woman has had to clean up more than a few awful messes.

There. The best of friends, I can assure you.

Please know that at the end of each chapter a list of rooms, suspects, and weapons is provided so that you may keep track of the shenanigans at the mansion during this visit.

Well, it's time to dive — rather, I should say, *ride* — into our first adventure together.

Do your best to keep your balance this weekend. Hang onto your hats — and your wallets!

Cheerio!

1.
Thief on Wheels

OVER THE YEARS, THERE HAD BEEN some strange sights at the Boddy Mansion, but none was stranger than the sight of Mr. Boddy careening into the Ball Room on a unicycle one morning, to the surprise of his weekend guests.

"Look!" said Professor Plum. "Someone's stolen the other half of Mr. Boddy's bicycle!"

"No, it's supposed to look that way," observed Miss Scarlet. "It's one of those what-do-you-call-its."

"What's a what-do-you-call-it?" asked a perplexed Professor Plum.

"It's called a unicycle," said Mr. Boddy. "I've been taking lessons."

"Is it difficult?" asked Mr. Green.

"You just have to learn to balance," said Mr. Boddy.

"Which is difficult, if you're as unbalanced as he is," snickered Mrs. White.

"Oh, Mrs. White," soothed Mr. Boddy. "You're still angry about the skid marks on the marble floors, aren't you?"

"It does make for more work around here," sighed Mrs. White.

"I, for one, find it very rude to ride a bicycle indoors!" said Mrs. Peacock.

"But this is a unicycle," Mr. Boddy pointed out.

"I don't care if it's a unicycle, a bicycle, or a tricycle! Regardless of the number of wheels, it's still rude!" insisted Mrs. Peacock.

"Perhaps," said Mr. Boddy. "But it's an awful lot of fun. I'm lucky to have a mansion big enough to ride around in."

A tired Mrs. White nodded her head. "Lucky for you, maybe. But *you* try scrubbing a skid mark that's a hundred feet long!"

"Say, could I have a try on that unicycle?" asked Mr. Green.

"Help yourself," Mr. Boddy replied.

It took several attempts for Mr. Green to get up on the unicycle seat. Then, as quickly as he got on, he fell off.

"This is hopeless," Mr. Green sighed. "The wheel keeps moving!"

"Maybe you need some training wheels," said Mrs. White with a smirk.

"Try pedaling as soon as you're up," suggested Mr. Boddy. "And put your arms out to the sides, for balance."

With some coaching, Mr. Green soon learned to handle the unicycle a bit better.

"It *is* fun!" he shouted with glee. "Now, if there

was only some way to make money doing this, it would be perfect."

"You could hire yourself out to entertain at children's birthday parties," suggested Miss Scarlet.

"I'd rather peddle these pedals," he replied.

"Let me try!" boomed Colonel Mustard. "Anything Mr. Green can do, I can do twice as well!"

"Colonel, if you're so good, why not ride a cycle with *no* wheels?" joked Mrs. Peacock.

"I want to go first," shouted Miss Scarlet, crowding to the front of the line. "If a man can ride that thing, it can't be too difficult."

"I'm so glad you're interested in the unicycle," said a beaming Mr. Boddy. "Because I've bought one for each of you. They're out in the Hall."

Mr. Boddy led his guests there. Sure enough, leaning against a wall were six unicycles, each with a different-colored seat.

"Please take the one with the seat color that matches your name," instructed Mr. Boddy.

A few minutes later . . .

A few minutes later, the guests wheeled their very own unicycles into the Ball Room.

Mr. Green's cycle had a green seat.

Colonel Mustard's cycle had a yellow seat.

Professor Plum's cycle sported a purple seat.

Mrs. Peacock's had a blue seat.

6

Mrs. White's had a white seat.

And Miss Scarlet's unicycle had a red seat.

"How does one get started?" asked Colonel Mustard.

"Put your right foot on the right pedal," explained Mr. Boddy, demonstrating on his own unicycle.

"Now jump up on the seat, put your left foot on the left pedal, and move the pedals back and forth for balance," he added.

"Sounds easy enough," said Colonel Mustard.

But as soon as he tried it, he fell backward and his unicycle skidded forward, leaving another mark on the floor for Mrs. White to clean up.

To his credit, Colonel Mustard tried again — and again — and again — and finally was able to balance atop the unicycle.

"Nothing to it," he assured the others.

Miss Scarlet was next. She, too, was able to keep her balance after a few tries.

"Hey, this is rather fun," observed Professor Plum. He was pedaling his unicycle in a tight circle and flapping his arms for balance.

In fact, all the guests but Mrs. White and Mrs. Peacock were doing quite well on their cycles.

But Mrs. White and Mrs. Peacock refused to try at all.

"It's undignified," protested Mrs. Peacock.

"It's bad enough I have to clean up your skid

marks," said Mrs. White. "Why would I wish to create some of my own, which I'd have to clean up, too?"

"Come on, you two. It's easy, once you get the hang of it," said Miss Scarlet. She was adeptly performing figure eights. "Just do what I do," she suggested.

"Maybe we should give it a try," Mrs. White said to Mrs. Peacock.

"No," replied Mrs. Peacock. "It's beyond rude."

"Perhaps," replied Mrs. White, "but think how fast you could get around the mansion."

"What good would that do?" snapped Mrs. Peacock.

"You could steal things and pedal away before anyone found out," whispered Mrs. White.

Mrs. Peacock considered this idea for several seconds. Then she leaped on her blue-seated cycle.

Several hours later . . .

Several hours later, after endless practicing, the guests could pedal about like experts.

All except for Mrs. White, who merely followed the others around, scrubbing tire marks off the floor.

Later that day . . .

8

Later that day, Mrs. Peacock pedaled out of the Ball Room and into the Study. There she stole a gold Candlestick and tucked it in her pocket.

She was about to ride out of the room when a guest rode in on the white-seated cycle.

"Hey," said Mrs. Peacock, "that's not your cycle."

"I know," said the guest, "but mine got a flat tire. Which explains why I have Mrs. White's cycle, but doesn't explain why you have Mr. Boddy's gold Candlestick. I saw you take it, and I want you to give it to me."

"Never!" refused Mrs. Peacock.

So the guest took out a Revolver.

"How about now?" the guest asked.

Mrs. Peacock handed over the Candlestick and rode away.

In the Hall she nearly ran into another guest who was riding his cycle.

"You should know," said Mrs. Peacock, "that someone seated on a white cycle has Mr. Boddy's gold Candlestick. If you're any sort of gentleman, you'll do something about it!"

"Perhaps I'll challenge the scoundrel to a duel," the other guest said, riding off to find the thief.

But once inside the Study he collided with a female guest.

"Now look what you've done!" she stormed, pointing to her smashed unicycle. "You've bent my rim!"

"If you don't lower your voice, I'll dent more than your rim," he threatened.

"You apologize!" she demanded.

"I'll do more than that," he said, backing off from a fight. "I'll give you my cycle."

"Why, thank you," she said.

He dropped his unicycle and took off on foot.

"His unicycle looks fine," she observed, "but I hate that awful seat color!"

Wanting her own color, she used the Wrench to remove her seat and put it on his cycle. Then she put the yellow seat on the smashed cycle and rode off on the working unicycle.

Meanwhile, the male guest found Mrs. Peacock riding around the Dining Room.

"Madam, I'm sorry to report that I can't find the Candlestick thief," he said.

"Try the Lounge," suggested Mrs. Peacock, quickly hiding the silver-plated Knife she had just swiped.

Then the guest on the purple-seated cycle pedaled into the Dining Room.

"Give me that Knife, Mrs. Peacock," he said.

"No, sir!" Mrs. Peacock refused.

"Have it your way, then," the man said.

He took out the Rope and threw a lasso around her. She and her unicycle fell to the floor with a crash.

Hearing the commotion, Colonel Mustard returned.

"That's no way to treat a proper lady like Mrs. Peacock," he said. "I challenge you to a duel!"

While the two engaged in bodily combat, Mrs. Peacock used the Knife to cut herself free and escaped on foot.

While this was going on, a female guest returned to the Study because her seat kept coming loose. Using the Wrench, she traded seats with the one on the smashed cycle once again.

Riding off, she crashed into someone who was still cleaning up tire marks.

In the confusion, the guest on the cycle switched her weapon for the Lead Pipe.

Mrs. Peacock was exhausted from walking around the mansion, so she returned for her cycle. Then she pedaled to the Lounge.

There she found a female guest threatening the Candlestick thief with the Lead Pipe.

But instead of Mrs. White's seat, the Candlestick thief's cycle now had the seat that was taken from the smashed cycle.

Mrs. Peacock took out her Knife and said to the thief, "You're through, you one-wheeled bandit."

WHO HAS THE CANDLESTICK?
WHAT COLOR SEAT WAS ON THE CYCLE
THE THIEF WAS RIDING?

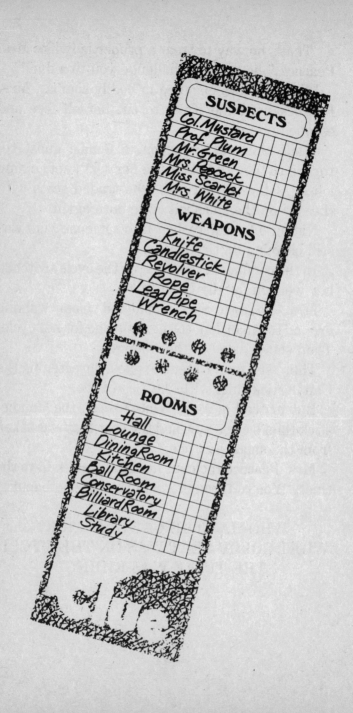

SOLUTION

MR. GREEN on the red-seated cycle

We know Mrs. White is not a suspect because she's cleaning tire marks. By process of elimination, we learn the identities of all the other guests except Mr. Green. Therefore, Mr. Green is the thief.

Mr. Green is riding Mrs. White's cycle, but he ends up with Miss Scarlet's red seat. After Miss Scarlet returned her seat to the smashed cycle, Mr. Green took the red seat and put it on Mrs. White's cycle.

When Mr. Boddy was alerted to the fiasco by his maid, he insisted that in the future all his guests would ride tricycles around the mansion so they'd be easier to keep track of.

2.
Shell Shock

MR. BODDY INVITED HIS GUESTS INTO the Conservatory one afternoon to see his latest rarity.

It was a strange, ribbed object that had the faint aroma of seawater.

Mr. Green tried to lift it, but the object was too heavy to move.

"What is it?" he asked. "A fossil of some sort?"

"No," said Mr. Boddy. "It's not a fossil. In fact, it was alive until a very short while ago."

"It looks like the world's largest paperweight," said Professor Plum. "Am I right?"

"You'll *sea* in a second," Mr. Boddy replied mysteriously.

"Mr. Boddy, I hope we don't have to *fish* around for an explanation," said Colonel Mustard. "I have a duel to fight at sundown."

"What type of duel is it this time?" asked Miss Scarlet. "Sabers? Pistols? Knives? Lead Pipes?"

"Revolvers," said Colonel Mustard. "So, Mr. Boddy, would you please hurry up?"

"*Shore* enough!"

14

"Is that some sort of a hint?" asked Mrs. Peacock.

Mr. Boddy nodded and said, "It's a *whale* of a treasure."

"I take it this . . . this *thing* came from the ocean," said Mr. Green.

Mr. Boddy again nodded. "This amazing specimen does, in fact, come from the sea. Now guess what it is."

"It's rude to have your guests *diving* for the answer," said Mrs. Peacock. "Especially when I need to be in the Lounge to await an important telephone call."

"Who's calling?" asked Miss Scarlet.

"The White House," said Mrs. Peacock proudly. "The President needs some advice on how to properly address a foreign dignitary."

"And I need to get back to the Kitchen," said Mrs. White, "where I'm sharpening all the cutlery."

"Mr. Boddy, is it the world's largest snail?" asked Professor Plum.

"My dear professor, I'm afraid you're much too slow," said Mr. Boddy. "It does come from the sea, but it's not a snail. Anyone else care to guess?"

"I'll *throw in my line* and give it a try," said a confident Mr. Green. "Is it some sort of gigantic, ship-eating monster?"

"No," answered Mr. Boddy.

"A rock, then?" asked Mr. Green.

"No," answered Mr. Boddy.

"A meteorite that fell from space?" guessed Mr. Green.

"You're way off space — I mean, base," answered Mr. Boddy.

"I know! The egg of some monstrous sea serpent!" said Mr. Green. "And it's about to hatch!"

"Wrong again," said Mr. Boddy. "Anyone else care to guess?"

No one cared to.

"You seem to be *floundering*," observed Mr. Boddy.

"Mr. Boddy, I think you're fooling us on *porpoise* — I mean, purpose," said Miss Scarlet.

"Mr. Boddy, quit *shrimping* on the hints," complained Mrs. White.

"Please don't be so *crabby*," said Mr. Boddy. "Let me give you a hint. This rarity belongs to the mollusk family."

"I know the Mollusk family," said Professor Plum. "Ollie and Molly and Polly and Wally and Dolly and little Solly Mollusk. Very nice people."

"Professor, would you please *clam* up?" asked Mrs. Peacock.

"Good guess, Mrs. Peacock!" said Mr. Boddy.

"It was?" she asked.

"Come on, you *chowder*heads," said Mr. Boddy. "Someone should be able to figure it out."

"I think I have," said Miss Scarlet.

"Go ahead," urged Mr. Boddy.

"Is it the world's largest oyster?" asked Miss Scarlet hopefully.

Mr. Boddy nodded. "Congratulations," he said.

"*Shucks*," moaned Mr. Green.

"That was a *fluke*," added Colonel Mustard. "How does Miss Scarlet know about oysters?"

"Two reasons," she said. "First, because one of my favorite families, the Rockefellers, had an oyster dish named after them. And second, because that's where pearls come from. And believe me," she added, "I know all about pearls."

"A pearl starts when a grain of sand gets inside an oyster and irritates it," explained Professor Plum.

"If I made a pearl every time someone irritated me, I'd be as rich as Rockefeller," joked Mr. Green.

A big smile lit up Miss Scarlet's face. "Mr. Boddy, does that thing contain the world's largest pearl?"

"Is it true?" asked an interested Mrs. White. "Do you now own the *mother of all pearls*?"

"If it is a pearl, I hope it's *cultured*," said Mrs. Peacock.

"Come back tomorrow morning and find out," Mr. Boddy told his guests. "Now, I'd like all of you to leave the room." He showed his guests the Conservatory door.

Several hours later . . .

17

Several hours later, a female guest sneaked into the room and tried to pry open the enormous oyster with the Wrench.

"Come on," she moaned. "Give up that pearl!"

While struggling to do so, she was interrupted by a male guest with the Lead Pipe.

"Ah, I see great minds think alike," he said. "If you let me help you, Miss Scarlet, we can steal the pearl together."

"Aren't you nice?" she said, hitting the intruder over the head with the Wrench. "So much for *your* great mind."

She dragged the body away, hiding it in a closet. Then she returned to the oyster.

"Oh, this bivalve is shut tight!" she groaned.

"Let me help," said another female guest, entering with the Knife.

"Did you come here from the Lounge?" the guest with the Wrench asked.

"Why would I do that?" asked the second female guest. She looked around the room. "I thought I saw Mr. Green come in here."

"You did," said the guest with the Wrench, hitting the other female guest over the head and taking her weapon.

"This is the weapon I needed in the first place," she said. The guest tried to work the blade of the Knife between the oyster's gigantic twin shells.

She tried for several minutes but couldn't get them to budge.

"Oh, this is ridiculous," she sighed. "This oyster won't ever give up its prize!"

"I know what will work," said a male guest, entering with the Candlestick.

"What?" asked the female guest.

"Heat," he said, holding the Candlestick under the enormous oyster.

"Are you sure it will work?" asked the female guest.

The male guest nodded. "In a few minutes, it will part its shells, and we can grab the pearl."

"Professor, you're a genius!" said the female guest, hitting him over the head with the Wrench. "But there's no 'we' when it comes to grabbing the pearl."

Still, even with heat, the gigantic oyster did not give up its enormous pearl.

Another female guest entered with the Rope. "I say we use this to hoist the oyster up high," she said. "Then we let go and hope the thing breaks open."

"That's a great suggestion," said the guest with the Wrench, hitting the other guest over the head.

The guest put down the Wrench, tied the Rope around the gigantic oyster, tossed the Rope over a large ceiling beam, and began to hoist it toward the ceiling.

Just then, a male guest entered, waving a weapon.

"Drop that Rope," he ordered.

"I don't think that's a good idea," she said.

"Do as I say," he demanded. "This instant!"

"Yes, sir," she said. "But you best stand clear."
She released the Rope.

The oyster fell to the ground with a loud crash.
The two gigantic shells split apart.

"Finally!" said the female guest, wiping the perspiration from her brow.

"Here, help me pull it further apart," said the
male guest.

Each of them pulled back on the gigantic shell.
Ever so slowly, the two halves creaked and separated.

"That's it!" said the female guest.

"I can see the pearl," said the male guest. "And,
believe me, it looks much too heavy to wear
around your neck."

"It's not quite loose yet," said the female guest.
"Keep working!"

Finally, after much struggle, a large pearl
spilled from the oyster.

"It's a beauty!" shouted the female guest.

It rolled across the floor.

The two guests dove for the enormous, flawless
pearl.

The slippery pearl slid ahead, out of the female
guest's grasp.

The male guest pounced on it, but the pearl
escaped his grasp, too.

Finally, the male guest chased the pearl until he was able to claim it as his prize.

WHO STOLE THE PEARL AND WITH WHICH WEAPON?

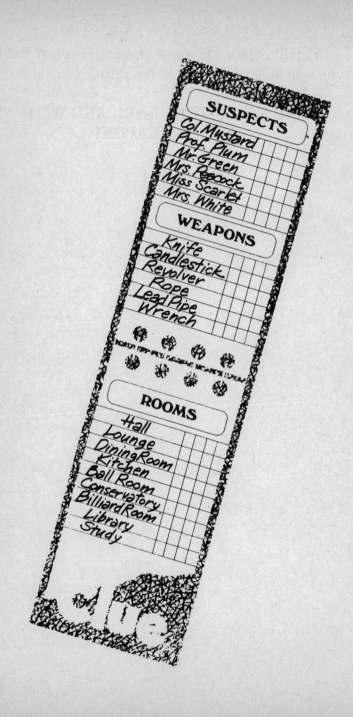

SUSPECTS

Col. Mustard
Prof. Plum
Mr. Green
Mrs. Peacock
Miss Scarlet
Mrs. White

WEAPONS

Knife
Candlestick
Revolver
Rope
Lead Pipe
Wrench

ROOMS

Hall
Lounge
Dining Room
Kitchen
Ball Room
Conservatory
Billiard Room
Library
Study

SOLUTION

COLONEL MUSTARD in the CONSERVATORY with the REVOLVER

We know that Colonel Mustard was the thief because the other male guests are referred to by name (Mr. Green) or title (Professor). We know he had the Revolver through process of elimination.

Fortunately, Mr. Boddy reclaimed the pearl, and the next day, Colonel Mustard had to make the world's largest pot of oyster stew to serve his host and fellow guests.

3.
Tennis, Anyone?

MR. BODDY CALLED HIS GUESTS INTO the Ball Room. There he was busily opening vacuum-sealed cans of tennis balls and writing a number on each ball.

"Tennis, anyone?" he asked.

"Are you planning an indoor tennis tournament?" asked Colonel Mustard.

"*Nyet!*" said Mr. Boddy.

"I don't see any net," said Professor Plum, looking around.

Mr. Boddy explained, "*Nyet* is Russian for 'no.' "

Miss Scarlet entered. "What is Mr. Boddy up to this time?" she asked.

"He's bouncing off the walls," replied Mrs. White.

Miss Scarlet turned to Mrs. White, and said, "I'm famished. Tell me, what is being served?"

"Tennis balls," Mrs. White replied.

"Well, I'm not *that* hungry," said Miss Scarlet.

"No, you don't understand," explained Mrs. White. "Mr. Boddy is serving tennis balls."

"I heard you the first time!" snapped Miss Scarlet. "And I refuse to eat them or any other sort of sporting equipment!"

Mrs. White rolled her eyes.

Mrs. Peacock entered and asked, "What is all this racket?"

Mr. Green picked up one of Mr. Boddy's hand-crafted, solid-titanium tennis racquets and swung it in the direction of Mrs. Peacock. "Here's one," he jested.

"How rude!" snapped Mrs. Peacock.

"Better yet, this one is strung with catgut," teased Mr. Green.

"Doubly rude!" said Mrs. Peacock.

"Good thing I wore the proper shoes," said Professor Plum, lifting up his trouser legs. "Sneakers."

"Sneakers are the perfect shoes for a thief," said a suspicious Mrs. White.

"Mr. Boddy, I demand you tell us what you're doing this instant," warned Colonel Mustard. He picked up a racquet and began to thrust it like a dueling sword. "If this scares you," he added, "wait until you see my backhand."

"Very well," said Mr. Boddy. "I thought you might enjoy a numbers lottery."

"What exactly is a numbers lottery?" asked Mrs. White.

"I've written a series of numbers on these tennis balls," explained Mr. Boddy.

Mr. Boddy then moved to a machine that had a large plastic tube coming out of it. The tube was pointed into the air. The machine was topped with a clear plastic dome.

"Next I shall put the balls inside my automatic tennis ball feeder," he went on.

He opened the dome lid and dropped the numbered balls inside.

"I can't remember the last time I felt such excitement," said Miss Scarlet with a smirk.

"I think we're just about ready," said Mr. Boddy. "Each of you must select from this bag a slip of paper with a number that matches one of those on a ball." He indicated a bag full of paper slips.

"What exactly does that machine do?" asked Professor Plum.

"I use this feeder to practice my tennis strokes. When I flick the switch, the feeder will bounce the balls around and release one. The guest whose number matches the released tennis ball will win a fabulous prize," concluded Mr. Boddy.

"And what is this fabulous prize?" asked Mrs. White with a yawn.

"The chance to watch me play in next week's all-county tennis tournament," announced a proud Mr. Boddy.

The guests started for the door.

"Excuse me," said Colonel Mustard. "I want out of here!"

"A numbers lottery. What a ridiculous idea," spouted Professor Plum.

"Move aside, and make it snappy. I'm first out of the door," snapped Mrs. Peacock, elbowing him back.

"Let me out of here before Boddy comes up with another dull idea," begged Mr. Green.

"Out of my way!" boomed Mrs. White.

"Hey, quit cutting in line!" warned Miss Scarlet.

But Mr. Boddy renewed their interest by adding, "The second part of the prize is a check for ten thousand dollars!"

"About face!" ordered Colonel Mustard.

"Mr. Boddy, I always thought a numbers lottery would be fun," said Professor Plum.

"We would never leave you alone," cooed Mrs. Peacock.

"Don't start without me," said Mr. Green.

"I'm back!" shouted Mrs. White.

"Tennis *is* my favorite game," said Miss Scarlet, hurrying back with the others. "Any game where zero equals *love* certainly fits my romantic nature."

"That's because you've loved more than a few zeroes in your life," chuckled Mr. Green.

"That from the man whose own mother labeled him a *double fault!*" she shot back.

"Will you two please stop it." said Mrs. Peacock. "Mr. Boddy is about to get started."

Mr. Boddy put the numbered tennis balls in the special machine. Then he lowered the dome and snapped it shut.

One by one, the guests picked slips of paper, each with a number.

Professor Plum drew the number 9.

Miss Scarlet drew the number 20.

Colonel Mustard drew the number 10.

Mrs. White drew the number 15.

Mrs. Peacock drew the number 5.

Mr. Green drew the number 12.

"Now may I flick the switch?" asked Mr. Boddy.

"Not so fast. I don't like my number," protested Miss Scarlet.

"Neither do I!" said Mrs. Peacock.

So, after asking Mr. Boddy for permission, they traded slips of paper.

"If they get to trade, I get to trade," insisted Mrs. White.

"Fine," said Mr. Boddy. "Who wants to trade with Mrs. White?"

Mr. Green raised his hand. "I will," he said.

So Mrs. White traded with Mr. Green.

"Well, I'm not about to be left out of this swapping business," said Colonel Mustard.

He traded numbers with Professor Plum.

"I think I liked my original number better," said Mr. Green. "Mrs. White, please trade back with me."

"Very well," she said.

"This new number is no better than my first one," said Colonel Mustard.

"Oh, give me yours, you silly man," said Mrs. Peacock, handing her slip to him.

"Is everyone finished?" asked Mr. Boddy.

The guests nodded.

But the instant that Colonel Mustard's back was turned, Miss Scarlet secretly switched numbers with him.

"Now, is everyone ready?" asked an ever-patient Mr. Boddy.

The guests clutched their individual numbers and nodded.

"I'll turn on the feeder," proclaimed Mr. Boddy.

He did so.

The feeder began to bounce the balls against the inside of the clear plastic lid. After a few suspenseful moments, it jettisoned a ball high into the air.

The guests followed its arc as the ball came within an inch of the Ball Room ceiling. Then it fell back toward the floor.

Mr. Boddy circled under the ball and caught it.

He looked at the winning number.

"Tell us!" demanded the guests.

"I won?" shouted Mr. Green. "Right?"

"No, *I* won!" said Mrs. Peacock.

"Make that check out to me!" insisted Mrs. White, waving her slip of paper.

"I know I'm the winner," said Professor Plum.

"Not so fast," Mr. Boddy said slyly. "First let's see how good you are at numbers."

"Numbers?" asked Colonel Mustard.

"Mrs. White, please pass out paper and pencils," said Mr. Boddy.

After she had done so, the guests were ready for Mr. Boddy's first hint.

"The winning number is divisible by five," said Mr. Boddy.

The guests used the paper and pencils to try to divide their numbers by five.

"Rats," said one guest, "I'm out!"

"So am I!" moaned a second guest.

"Well, I'm still in the running for that ten thousand dollar check," said a third, happy guest.

"The winning number is divisible by three," Mr. Boddy said as his second hint.

The remaining contestants tried to divide their numbers by three.

One guest said, "Darn it! I'm sunk!"

Another guest moaned, "Looks like my number is also eliminated."

A third guest said, "It's not fair!"

"What's not fair?" asked Mr. Boddy.

"That I lost, too!" said the guest, tearing up the slip of paper.

"Well, I have the winner!" said the remaining person, waving the matching slip of paper.

WHO IS THE WINNER?

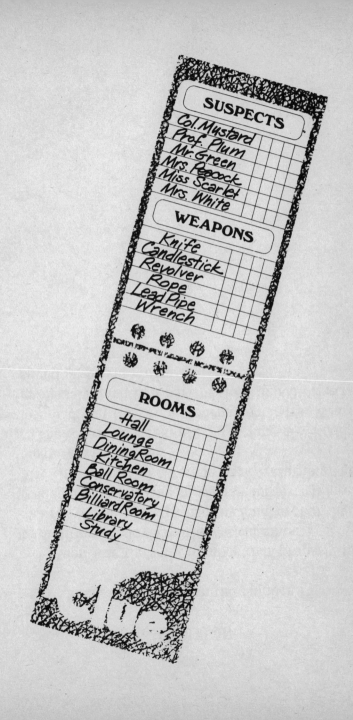

SOLUTION

MRS. WHITE, with the number 15

Fifteen was the only number that properly fit both of Mr. Boddy's mathematical hints.

Mrs. White originally had the number, but then traded it with Mr. Green. Luckily for Mrs. White, Mr. Green decided to trade back, returning the lucky number to her.

The following week, after watching Mr. Boddy lose badly at the tennis tournament, Mrs. White graciously gave him part of the $10,000 prize to spend on private lessons.

4.
Knock Around the Clock

WHEN PROFESSOR PLUM AND MR. Green entered the Hall one evening, at Mr. Boddy's request, they were astounded by what they saw. The room was filled with hundreds and hundreds of clocks.

"I guess we got here just in time," said Mr. Green.

"My gosh, Mr. Boddy," said Professor Plum, "have you collected every clock in the entire country?"

"No," said Mr. Boddy. "These timepieces are from my own rather extensive collection."

"They're yours?" asked an astonished Professor Plum.

"They're my hour collection," replied Mr. Boddy.

"They're yours — or ours?" asked a confused Professor Plum.

"They're *my* hour collection," repeated Mr. Boddy.

"Let's throw one out the window and see how time flies," suggested Mr. Green.

Mr. Boddy was not amused.

"How'd you find time to collect all these clocks?" asked Professor Plum.

"By making every minute count," admitted Mr. Boddy.

"Now you have plenty of time on your hands," observed Mr. Green. He picked up one old timepiece and examined it closely.

"Don't drop it," advised Professor Plum. "You wouldn't want to kill time."

"Well," said Mr. Green, putting the clock back on a shelf. "I have to say that Mr. Boddy's collection is *second* to none."

"Collecting clocks," mused Professor Plum. "Talk about a *cuckoo* habit."

"And guess who gets to dust every last one of those ticking monsters," said Mrs. White, joining the others.

"Better *watch* it," Mr. Boddy advised her, "or it may be time for a new job."

"Sorry I'm late," said a winded Colonel Mustard, entering, "but my watch stopped. Would any of you happen to have the right time?"

"Look around, Colonel!" snapped Mr. Green. "Is your mind ticking at all?"

Colonel Mustard finally noticed that he was surrounded by clocks, all of which read 9:15.

"Ah, nine-fifteen," he said, adjusting his wristwatch. "Thank you very much."

"It's nine-fifteen standard time, to be precise,"

34

Mr. Boddy said, checking his pocket watch against the other timepieces in the room.

Miss Scarlet entered. "When I heard all that ticking," she said, "I was afraid there was a bomb in here."

"A time bomb?" grinned Colonel Mustard.

"Nothing so dramatic," said Mr. Green. "Just Mr. Boddy's clock collection."

"And pray tell, why are you all standing here?" asked Miss Scarlet. "Is Mr. Boddy going to make time stop?"

"Make time stop?" repeated Professor Plum. "That's impossible!"

"Obviously, you've never been in love," sighed Miss Scarlet. "You still haven't explained why you asked us all here," she said to Mr. Boddy.

"Because tonight's the night we change from standard time to daylight savings time," explained Mr. Boddy.

"Ah, that explains the feeling of intrigue and excitement in the air," joked Miss Scarlet.

"You mean, at this time tomorrow night it will be ten-fifteen instead of nine-fifteen?" asked Colonel Mustard. "And I'll have to adjust my watch *again*?"

"Exactly," said Mr. Boddy.

"Colonel, your life is one little tragedy after another, isn't it?" kidded Mr. Green.

"Quiet, sir, or I'll *clean your clock*," threatened Colonel Mustard.

"Gentlemen, please," pleaded Mr. Boddy. "Let's not get distracted from the important task at hand."

"And that is?" asked Mrs. White.

"Tonight after midnight, each and every clock must be reset one hour ahead," said Mr. Boddy.

All eyes turned to Mr. Boddy's loyal maid.

"And let me guess who gets to reset all these clocks," said Mrs. White with a sigh.

"I'm sorry, Mrs. White," said Mr. Boddy. "There are a lot of clocks, it's true."

"And each one has a different face," observed Miss Scarlet.

"In that case," said Mr. Green, looking around the room, "Mr. Boddy isn't just two-faced. He's more like two-hundred-faced!"

"Please accept my apologies for being late," said Mrs. Peacock as she finally joined the others. "Have I missed anything?"

"Mr. Boddy is showing us his collection of rocks — I mean, clocks," replied Professor Plum. "We've having the time of our lives!"

"Are any of these clocks particularly valuable?" asked Mr. Green, continuing his inspection.

Mr. Boddy looked over his collection. "Of course, they're all irreplaceable. But you're asking which one is particularly valuable?"

After a thorough search, he pointed to a small statue of a woman. Strangely, it had a clock where the woman's stomach should be, and a large ruby in the middle, where her navel should be.

"I'd say it — or, rather, she — is my most valuable timepiece," said a proud Mr. Boddy.

"How rude!" snapped Mrs. Peacock. "Whoever made that thing should be *clocked*!"

"Madam, please don't get *ticked* off. It's an antique from the seventeenth century," said Mr. Boddy.

"Just because it's old doesn't necessarily mean it has any value," said Miss Scarlet. "I mean, look at Mrs. Peacock. My gentlemen callers wouldn't give her the time of day."

"How rude!" said Mrs. Peacock.

"Go on, Mr. Boddy," said an interested Mr. Green. "You were telling us about this special clock."

"The face is encrusted with diamonds," said Boddy. "The hair is streaked with silver. The eyes are sapphires and the hands are gold."

"And the feet?" asked Professor Plum.

Mr. Boddy looked at Professor Plum and rolled his eyes. "Maybe the professor needs a time-out," he said.

"Well, this has been a fascinating evening," said Miss Scarlet, eyeing the valuable antique.

"Yes," agreed Mr. Green, thinking of ways to steal the precious clock himself.

Mrs. Peacock pretended to cover a yawn. "I'm

ready for a good night's sleep," she said. But she was working on her own plan to take the antique.

"My dear guests," said Mr. Boddy, "please be informed that the mansion's security system will be temporarily turned off at two A.M. standard time for adjustment."

"Why tonight?" asked Mr. Green.

"Because it's time for its seasonal adjustment," said Mr. Boddy.

Colonel Mustard's eyes twinkled.

Professor Plum smiled slyly.

"Now," Mr. Boddy concluded, "all of us should leave Mrs. White to her task."

Mr. Boddy led everyone else from the room.

Knowing she would be left alone with the priceless antique, Mrs. White checked her apron to make certain the Revolver was there.

Several hours later . . .

Several hours later, Mrs. White finished the enormous task of resetting all of the clocks.

"It's about time!" she said with a sigh.

She went to find Mr. Boddy and his guests in the Lounge. They were watching reruns of the old TV series *Beat the Clock*.

"It's awfully late," she informed them, "and I'm turning in."

"You're turning into what?" asked Professor Plum.

Mrs. White was about to say something, but instead she simply said, "Good night!" She and the other guests went to bed.

In their own rooms, each guest set an alarm clock to go off in a few hours, though one guest did *not* adjust the time to daylight saving.

A few hours later . . .

A few hours later, alarm clocks went off all over the mansion. Mrs. White was the first down the stairs.

She made certain that the mansion security system was truly turned off.

It was turned off.

"Time to get going," she said to herself.

She was about to take out her weapon — when she was attacked by a male guest with the Rope.

"Forgive me for tying you down," he said.

The male guest left White in a series of knots. Then he stole the priceless antique clock and fled to the Study, where he planned to hide it.

But he was attacked by another guest with the Candlestick.

"Let me take that off your hands," the guest with the Candlestick said.

The guest with the Candlestick took the antique clock and rushed into the Conservatory.

There he was attacked by a guest with the Knife.

The guest with the Knife took the antique clock and crossed to the Billiard Room.

"Maybe I have time for a quick game," he said.

But another guest jumped him from behind and attacked him with the Wrench. This guest took the antique clock to the Dining Room.

"Time for a little repast?" she wondered to herself.

But before she could sit down and enjoy a snack, she was attacked by a guest with the Lead Pipe.

The guest with the Lead Pipe took the antique clock to the Kitchen, where it was successfully hidden.

Upstairs, hearing the commotion, Mr. Boddy woke up.

He checked his bedside clock. It read 3:15 A.M. daylight saving time.

Immediately Mr. Boddy ran from his room and checked his guests' bedrooms. He found each and every one empty.

"I knew it," he whispered. "Some or all of my guests are after my antique clock."

Instead of investigating, though, he decided to wait until morning.

The next morning . . .

The next morning, Mr. Boddy called his guests into the Hall. "Last night one of you stole my antique clock," he said.

"It wasn't me," said Mrs. White.

"Nor I!" insisted Professor Plum.

Before the other guests could make excuses, Mr. Boddy asked each of them where he or she had been at precisely 3:15 A.M.

Each of the guests answered truthfully, and one of them said, "I was back in bed sound asleep."

"I know who stole my antique clock," concluded Mr. Boddy.

WHO STOLE THE ANTIQUE CLOCK?

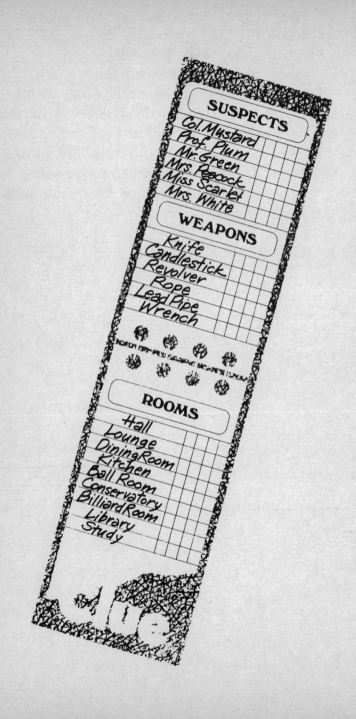

SOLUTION

MRS. PEACOCK

The solution lies in the early part of the story. Only one guest was not present when the time change to daylight saving was discussed, and that guest was Mrs. Peacock. Therefore, only she would truthfully say she was asleep at 3:15 A.M. (which was actually 2:15 A.M. standard time) because she didn't know to set her clock ahead by one hour.

To make up for her crime, poor Mrs. Peacock volunteered to dust all the clocks until the ticking almost drove her crazy.

5.
The Rosy Scarecrow

IT WAS A LOVELY, SUNNY MORNING, but the guests could not find Mr. Boddy.

"Perhaps he's on the mansion roof, sunning himself," suggested Miss Scarlet. "That's what I'd be doing on such a glorious day."

But Mr. Boddy was not on the roof.

"I'll bet he's perfecting his golf swing at the mansion's driving range," said Mr. Green. "On a day like today, I'd be on the green myself."

But Mr. Boddy was not at the driving range.

"Well, that really *tees* me off!" stormed Mr. Green.

"I imagine he's off driving through the countryside in one of his roadsters," said Mrs. Peacock. "Taking in the sights on such a lovely morning."

But all of Mr. Boddy's many luxury automobiles were in the garage.

"Perhaps he's doing a few laps in the swimming pool," Colonel Mustard thought out loud.

However, when the guests arrived at the pool, it was empty.

Professor Plum wiped some sweat from his brow. "If I were Mr. Boddy — and I know I'm not — on such a warm morning, I would be enjoying some fresh-squeezed lemonade in the Kitchen," he said.

The guests rushed to the Kitchen, but it, too, was empty.

"As long as we're here, we might as well enjoy some lemonade," said Professor Plum with a shrug of his shoulders.

He opened the refrigerator and poured glasses of lemonade for all of the guests.

"You don't think that he has left us alone in the mansion?" asked Miss Scarlet, sipping the cool drink.

"It would not be like Boddy to go off and not tell anyone," added Mrs. Peacock. "That would be a display of very bad manners!"

"Perhaps there's some way we can still salvage the day. After all, if Boddy is gone, we're free to take what we wish!" said Colonel Mustard.

Just as the guests were about to embark on some early morning looting, Mrs. White entered the Kitchen.

"No such luck," said Mrs. White.

"Do you know where our host is?" asked Miss Scarlet.

Mrs. White nodded. "He's out in the garden, pruning his prize-winning roses."

The guests headed off to the garden. Sure enough, Mr. Boddy was there. He was dressed in overalls and a straw gardening hat.

"Good morning," said Mrs. Peacock.

"Good morning," said Colonel Mustard.

"Or, as we say in France, *bonjour*," said Miss Scarlet.

But Mr. Boddy didn't answer.

"How rude!" snorted Mrs. Peacock.

"Show a little respect, man," threatened Colonel Mustard, "or I'll challenge you to a duel!"

Suddenly, Mr. Green began laughing hysterically.

"What's so funny?" asked Miss Scarlet.

"Yes, please share the joke," added Professor Plum.

"That isn't Mr. Boddy," laughed Mr. Green, pointing to the object in the overalls and straw hat. "It's a scarecrow!"

"That's impossible," said Colonel Mustard. "I've known Mr. Boddy for years, so don't tell me I don't recognize him!"

Upon closer inspection, however, the guests discovered that the figure in hat and overalls was, indeed, a scarecrow.

"I should have known it was a scarecrow," said Professor Plum.

"If you only had a brain," observed Mrs. White.

"So, this can mean just one thing. Mr. Boddy is still missing," concluded Colonel Mustard.

"We all know what *that* means," added Miss Scarlet, with a smile.

The other guests nodded. They were about to head back to the mansion and do a little polite pilfering when the real Mr. Boddy emerged from the nearby gardening shed with a watering can.

"Good morning!" he called. "Lovely day for gardening."

"If your idea of fun is pulling weeds," said Mrs. White.

"They thought the scarecrow was you," explained Mr. Green.

"Well," said Professor Plum, "it is a good likeness. Except for the hay sticking out of the ears."

Mr. Boddy laughed. "I put that fellow up to keep the birds away from my flowers and vegetables. My roses are very valuable."

"They are?" asked Miss Scarlet, perking up at once.

"Tell us about them!" said Colonel Mustard, moving closer.

"They are a special hybrid I developed all on my own," explained Mr. Boddy. "They're called Blue Boddy Beauties."

"Are you blue?" asked Professor Plum.

"Actually, my roses make me especially happy," said Mr. Boddy.

"What's so special about them?" asked Mrs. Peacock.

"Well," continued Mr. Boddy, "besides their

lovely blue color, they bloom only when the moon is full."

"Blue roses!" said a doubtful Miss Scarlet. "I've never heard of such a thing. My many gentlemen callers always bring me red, pink, or yellow roses."

"Blue roses?" said Colonel Mustard. "Ridiculous! A rose by any other name — or color — would smell as sweet."

"The colonel is correct," said Professor Plum. "A rose is a rose is a rose."

"Mine are special," insisted Mr. Boddy. "And they'll be blooming blue tonight — because the moon is full."

Professor Plum looked worried.

"What's the matter?" asked Mr. Boddy.

"I know this is a thorny notion, but I thought vegetation required solar power to bloom, not lunar power," said Professor Plum.

"Boddy is a lunar-tick," said Mrs. White.

"That's what makes my roses so special, and so sought after," said Mr. Boddy. "The Society of Unusual Roses has been badgering me to sell them my plants for fifty thousand dollars."

"Fifty thousand!" whistled Mr. Green. "That certainly puts the blush back on the rose!"

"Fifty thousand dollars? Does that include the box and ribbon?" asked Professor Plum.

"Fifty thousand for roses?" said Miss Scarlet. "Why don't you sell?"

"When I've perfected my rosebushes," Mr. Boddy explained, "I plan to give them away. Beauty should be shared for free!"

"A very proper notion," remarked Mrs. Peacock, busily working up a plan to steal the roses.

"If I were you, I'd dig up those roses and sell them, keep most of the money, and just give a little bit away. Think of those plants as an investment," urged Mr. Green, getting out his pocket calculator.

"No," insisted Mr. Boddy. "These roses stay right here. But if you wish, you're all invited to join me when the moon comes up to witness the blooming of the Blue Boddy Beauties."

The guests eyed one another expectantly and began to devise their evil plans.

Later that night . . .

Later that night, right before moonrise, a man exited the mansion and tiptoed out to the garden. He held the Knife, which he intended to use to cut the valuable roses.

But just as he reached the garden, he was knocked over the head with the Lead Pipe. A woman took the Knife and the Lead Pipe and tiptoed toward the blue roses.

She was bending carefully over the rosebushes and preparing to take a cutting when she was knocked aside by another guest.

"Too blooming bad," the attacker said to the woman as he tied her up with the Rope, "but those roses are mine."

He took the Lead Pipe, but forgot the Knife, which was lying right beside the tied-up woman. Then he attempted to use the Lead Pipe to dig up a rosebush.

But he was interrupted by Miss Scarlet, who pointed the Revolver at the man.

"Drop the Lead Pipe, Colonel, and move away from the roses or I'll shoot," she said.

He did as Miss Scarlet instructed. In fact, he kept backing away from her until he was all the way back at the mansion.

Miss Scarlet was about to uproot a rosebush when the guest who was tied up cut the Rope with the Knife and freed herself.

Sneaking up on the flower bed, she used the Rope to pull Miss Scarlet away from the plants. The two began to struggle, when a voice stopped them.

"Does either of you have a light? I brought the Candlestick out to see the lunar-powered blooming, but I forgot a match. I always seem to forget things. . . ." said the voice.

Miss Scarlet lit a match, temporarily blinding the guest with the Candlestick.

When he shielded his eyes from the glare, she clocked him over the head with her weapon.

But just then, Mrs. Peacock screamed, "Ay-eeeeeeeeee!" She dropped the Knife.

"What is it?" asked Miss Scarlet, picking up the Knife.

"The scarecrow moved!" whispered Mrs. Peacock.

The guests studied the scarecrow, which was wearing overalls and a straw hat. It stood motionless in the moonlight.

"You're seeing things," said Miss Scarlet.

She bent down to cut a rose with the Knife when the scarecrow tapped her on the shoulder.

Miss Scarlet screamed.

"I wouldn't if I were you," whispered the scarecrow, waving a weapon. "I want all of you to move away this instant. My job is to protect these roses, and I'll stop at nothing to do just that!"

"It must be Mr. Boddy dressed up again as the scarecrow," insisted Mrs. Peacock.

But it wasn't Mr. Boddy.

The frightened guests ran screaming back to the mansion.

WHO IS THE SCARECROW?
WHAT WEAPON DOES THE SCARECROW
HAVE?

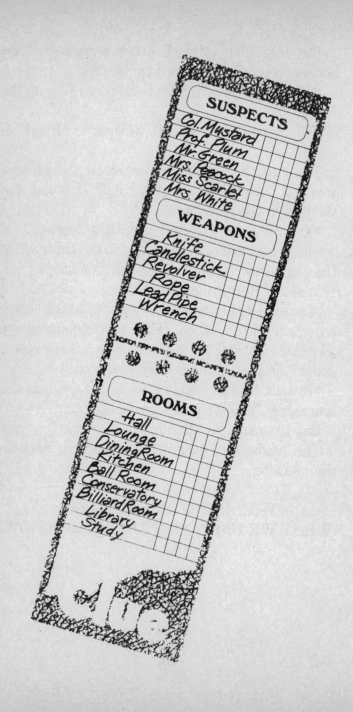

SOLUTION

MRS. WHITE is the scarecrow. She has the WRENCH.

A male guest was knocked out by a female guest with the Knife, who we later learn was Mrs. Peacock. Colonel Mustard and Miss Scarlet are identified by name, and Professor Plum is identified by his forgetfulness and musings about lunar power. Since Colonel Mustard and Professor Plum are eliminated, we can eliminate the first male guest as Mr. Green. This leaves Mrs. White — who cleverly dressed up as the scarecrow — holding the only weapon not previously mentioned.

Luckily for her, Mrs. White was able to convince Mr. Boddy that she impersonated the scarecrow to protect his roses — *not* to steal them. But Mr. Boddy was forced to install an electric steel fence around his garden to protect his priceless blue roses.

6.
Bad Hare Day

MR. BODDY AND HIS GUESTS WERE having a leisurely lunch in the Dining Room, except for poor Mrs. White. She had to make each of the picky guests an individual entree, except for one dish that Mr. Boddy insisted they all share.

Colonel Mustard wanted pork chops and a baked potato smothered with sour cream and chives. "It's a manly meal for a manly man," he had told Mrs. White.

Miss Scarlet wanted a low-calorie endive salad. "Serve it with low-calorie salad dressing, whole wheat bread, and nonfat butter, and I want my decaffeinated coffee with nondairy creamer," she had instructed Mrs. White.

"If you want to cut down on calories and fat, why not skip lunch altogether?" suggested Mrs. White.

Mr. Green wanted a sirloin steak served with corn on the cob. "It's the lunch preferred by millionaires," he boasted.

Professor Plum wanted poached fish served with rice. "Good nutrition for the brain," he said.

Mrs. Peacock would eat only watercress and cucumber sandwiches with the crusts carefully removed from the bread. "Crust is so rude," she insisted.

And Mr. Boddy had his usual midday fare: lobster salad served with avocado and beefsteak tomatoes.

An exhausted Mrs. White wheeled the various dishes into the Dining Room on a cart. "I hope you're all happy," she said.

"Aren't you eating?" asked Mr. Boddy.

"What I'm doing is resting," she said, collapsing in a chair at the far end of the table.

Mr. Boddy was the first to finish his lunch. Then he took a strange object from his pocket.

"What is that?" asked a startled Mrs. White. "And please don't tell me that thing is going to eat, too."

"It's a keychain," said Mr. Boddy. "And no, Mrs. White, it won't mean more work for you."

"It looks like the paw of some small animal," observed Professor Plum.

"It is," said Mr. Boddy. "Or, more exactly, it was."

"An animal was killed so you could have that trinket?" asked Miss Scarlet. "I think it's heartless. Unless, of course, someone is offering me a mink coat."

"How rude!" exclaimed Mrs. Peacock. "Bringing *that* to the table. Mr. Boddy, you should be sent to your room."

"Did you hunt down a wild beast and take home a trophy?" asked a hopeful Colonel Mustard.

"Actually, this was sent to me by my aunt Bunny," Mr. Boddy explained.

"Aunt Bunny who's married to your uncle Bugs?" asked Mr. Green.

"The very woman," said Mr. Boddy with a nod. "Bugs and Bunny have a carrot farm not far from here. She was nice enough to send me this antique rabbit's foot."

"Antique rabbit's foot?" repeated Professor Plum. "How unusual."

"It's disgusting!" said Miss Scarlet.

"A rabbit's foot?" said Mr. Green with a chuckle. "I had one of those as a boy. I sold it years later for a tidy profit, I remember."

"It's a good luck charm," said Mr. Boddy.

"Like a horseshoe," added Professor Plum. "Or a four-leaf clover."

"Precisely," said Mr. Boddy with a nod.

"I can tell you, Mr. Boddy," interrupted Colonel Mustard, "it's a worthless trinket. Junk."

"Yes, please remove that thing from the premises this instant," insisted Mrs. Peacock.

"Its chain is solid gold," said Mr. Boddy. "Worth thousands of dollars."

"A solid-gold chain? How lucky!" cooed Miss Scarlet. "I think it's cute! Here, bunny, bunny."

"Yes," agreed Professor Plum, getting up from his seat. "Let me hop on over for a closer look."

Professor Plum examined the chain, then announced, "I have a hutch — I mean, hunch — that it's quite genuine."

"A twenty-four *carrot* gold chain?" joked Mr. Green.

"You need to guard that very carefully," warned Mrs. White, cleaning away the lunch dishes. "You know what they say about a priceless rabbit's foot — 'Hare today, gone tomorrow.' "

"That's so *bunny* that I forgot to laugh," sneered Colonel Mustard, gnawing on a bone.

Mr. Boddy patted his stomach, then pushed his chair back from the table. "Please excuse me. I'm heading upstairs to hop into bed for my afternoon nap," he said.

Before leaving, Mr. Boddy added, "Mrs. White, thank you for a splendid lunch. Especially the one dish you made for all of us to enjoy."

"Yes," said Mrs. Peacock, dabbing her mouth with a linen napkin. "It was Welsh rarebit, correct?"

"Don't you mean Welsh *rabbit*?" joked Mrs. White.

An hour later . . .

An hour later, a female guest with the Lead Pipe sneaked into Mr. Boddy's room.

Creeping toward the bed, she was prepared to

use the weapon. But she didn't have to because Mr. Boddy was snoring away.

"Did you count bunnies to help you fall asleep?" she softly whispered.

The guest took the priceless rabbit's foot from the nightstand and tiptoed out of Mr. Boddy's room.

She then walked down the stairs to the main floor. There, the guest stopped in the Hall, thinking she could hide the rabbit's foot in the grandfather clock.

"Excuse me," another guest said, surprising her.

The thief turned around with a start. "Yes?" she replied, hiding the rabbit's foot behind her back.

"You haven't seen Mr. Boddy, have you?" the second guest asked.

"I believe he's upstairs, napping," the thief answered.

"Very good," the guest said. "By the way, do you have the time?"

"Do I have the time for what?" the thief asked.

"I mean, do you know what time it is?" the guest asked.

"Professor, there's a grandfather clock right here!"

The thief turned around to point it out and was attacked by the male guest with the Wrench. The rabbit's foot fell from her grasp.

"Looks like it's your *unlucky* day," the male guest said.

He reached down and picked up the rabbit's foot, and then went to the Study.

But on second thought, he left the Study and went into the Lounge.

Resigned, the original thief struggled to her feet. She felt an enormous bump forming on her head. "My hair stylist won't like this," she said. She shrugged her shoulders and headed for the Conservatory.

In the Lounge, the new thief found a male guest throwing the Knife against a wooden target.

"Practicing for your next duel?" the thief asked.

"One's skills with a knife should remain sharp," the guest with the Knife said. "By the way, do you know if Mr. Boddy is still napping?"

"Last I heard," the thief said.

"How lucky for me," the guest concluded.

He attacked the thief with the Knife and stole the rabbit's foot. He took it into the empty Billiard Room.

He was about to hide it when he heard someone approaching, so he fled into the Library. There he found someone dusting Mr. Boddy's books.

"What do you want?" she asked.

"Oh, I was looking for something to read," the thief lied.

The other person nodded. "Yes, it'll be a cold

day when one of you helps me clean up the mansion."

The thief moved to the shelf. "Does Mr. Boddy own a copy of *Rabbit Hill*, *Peter Cottontail*, *The Runaway Bunny*, *The Velveteen Rabbit*, or *Rabbit, Run*?"

"Why the sudden interest in things with floppy ears?" the dusting person asked.

"Oh, no reason," the thief said.

He started to browse the shelves when he was attacked and tied up with the Rope.

"Try hopping now," the attacker mocked.

The attacker took the rabbit's foot and went into the Conservatory. There she found another female guest watching a soap opera on TV.

"These tales of love make my heart go thumpity-thump," said the guest.

"I'm so hoppy — I mean, *happy* — for you," said the thief.

"Do you have any idea whether Mr. Boddy is still asleep?" the TV-watching guest asked.

"I have no idea, but I imagine so," said the thief.

"Good," said the TV watcher, attacking the thief with the Candlestick.

The thief fell to the ground and let go of the rabbit's foot. The guest picked it up and held it close.

"It was mine first, anyway!" she said.

She rushed into the Dining Room, but felt uneasy since that was where the rabbit's foot was first discussed. So she ventured on into the Kitchen.

"How rude to rush in here!" snapped a guest munching on a carrot stick.

"Sorry, wrong room," said the thief, leaving.

She tried the remaining room.

But there the remaining guest lay in wait.

That guest, using the remaining weapon, murdered the thief and ended up with the rabbit's foot.

WHO WAS THE LAST TO STEAL THE RABBIT'S FOOT?

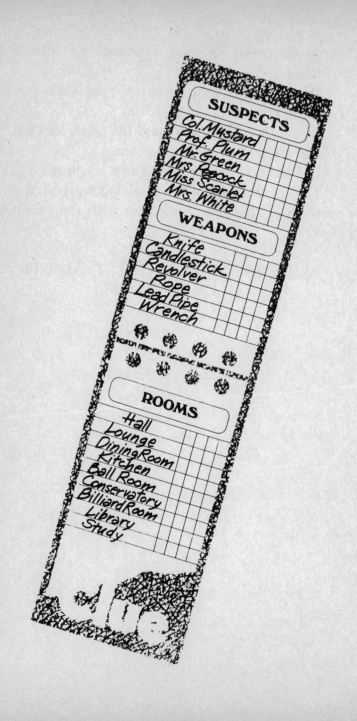

SOLUTION

MR. GREEN in the BALL ROOM with the REVOLVER

The references to Professor, duels, dusting, and rudeness eliminate Professor Plum, Colonel Mustard, Mrs. White, and Mrs. Peacock. This leaves Miss Scarlet as the first and last female thief, and Mr. Green as the murderer.

By using the process of elimination, all possibilities but the Ball Room and Revolver are accounted for.

It turned out to be Miss Scarlet's and Mr. Boddy's lucky day, after all. The bullet merely grazed Miss Scarlet, and the sound of the gunshot woke Mr. Boddy, who caught Mr. Green with the rabbit's foot. It wasn't such a lucky day for Mr. Green, however. He had to clean Mr. Boddy's rabbit hutches for a month.

7.
Dark Side of the Moon

IN THE LIBRARY ONE NIGHT, MR. Boddy was studying a book on astronomy.

"Just as I thought," he said to himself. "Tonight's the night!"

He called his guests into the room.

"Ladies and gentlemen," he said, "tonight we shall be privileged to witness one of the natural world's greatest and rarest shows."

"I hope you're not showing us the video of you lifting weights," said Miss Scarlet.

"Is a volcano about to erupt in the vicinity?" asked Colonel Mustard.

"Turn your gaze heavenward," suggested Mr. Boddy.

Professor Plum did so. "Is the ceiling going to fall in?" he asked.

"No, I'm referring to the night sky," hinted Mr. Boddy.

"Good heavens," said Mrs. White. "Don't tell me that tonight a supernova will explode."

"No," said Mr. Boddy.

"Let me offer a guess. We're about to be visited

by aliens in strange-looking spaceships?" asked Mrs. White.

"I think not," said Mr. Boddy.

"Good," said Mrs. White, "because we're just about out of food."

"The aliens could always eat the moon," joked Miss Scarlet. "It's made of green cheese."

"No, it isn't," said Professor Plum. "And, besides, even an alien wouldn't dare eat cheese that had turned green."

"You're close, Miss Scarlet," said Mr. Boddy.

"Something to do with the moon?" she asked.

Mr. Boddy nodded.

"How romantic," she said. "Are you going to serenade us with some of the wonderful music written about the moon? Starting with 'Moonlight Serenade'? Then moving on to 'Moon River'?"

"It's more spectacular than a simple song," said Mr. Boddy.

"You're not taking us all to the moon?" asked Colonel Mustard. "Have you rented a rocket ship?"

"My word, no!" said Mr. Boddy with a chuckle.

"Too bad," said Colonel Mustard. "Due to the lighter gravity there, I might be able to fight a duel with myself."

"Please tell us," said Mrs. Peacock, "before the night is over."

"As you wish. I'm referring to tonight's lunar eclipse," said Mr. Boddy.

"Lunar eclipse?" asked Mrs. White.

"Due to the earth's moving between the sun and the moon, the earth's shadow will cast the moon into complete darkness," explained Professor Plum. "It's a very rare occurrence."

"Rarer than you having your facts straight?" asked Mrs. White.

"When it happened in ancient times, people believed the gods were angry," added Colonel Mustard.

"Yes," said Mr. Green. "I read something about it. Strange things can happen during a lunar eclipse."

"You're right," said Mrs. Peacock, holding the Candlestick. "Earthquakes happen and volcanoes are prone to erupt during eclipses."

"Oh, stop such silly talk. I, for one, do not believe in such superstitions," boasted Miss Scarlet. "Nothing strange will happen tonight."

"Are you sure?" asked Professor Plum.

"I'd bet my life on it!" insisted Miss Scarlet.

"Be careful what you're willing to bet," warned Colonel Mustard.

"Well, I'm sleeping with the Lead Pipe tonight, just in case," said Mr. Green.

Miss Scarlet laughed at him. "In case the man in the moon tries to bother you?"

"And here's my protection," said Mrs. White, holding the Revolver.

"And I'm taking no chances," added Colonel Mustard, holding the Wrench.

Miss Scarlet couldn't believe how the other guests were acting.

"Colonel, be polite and trade weapons with me," said Mrs. Peacock.

Colonel Mustard was happy to oblige.

"And I'd like to trade with you, Mr. Green," said Mrs. White.

"Certainly," said Mr. Green.

"What a bunch of cowards!" sneered Miss Scarlet.

"Ladies and gentlemen, please," begged Mr. Boddy. "There's no need to worry."

"Speak for yourself," whispered Professor Plum, holding the Knife.

"Moon or no moon, I'm not afraid," proclaimed Miss Scarlet.

"Prove it," challenged Mr. Green.

"Very well." She took out the Rope. "To prove it, I'll tie myself to a chair in clear view of the eclipse," she said. "Come morning, I invite you to see how well I survived the night."

"She's such a braggart," one guest whispered to another.

"Someone should cut Miss Scarlet down to size!" agreed the second guest.

Later that night . . .

Later that night, Miss Scarlet positioned a chair near a window in one of the mansion's rooms, and she tied herself to it.

Mr. Boddy entered and checked the knots.

"They're good and secure," he assured her.

"Do the other guests know which room I'm in?" asked Miss Scarlet.

"No, that's our secret," Mr. Boddy told her.

After wishing Miss Scarlet good night, Mr. Boddy left the room.

Miss Scarlet contentedly looked out the window, humming "Moon Dance" to herself. After that, she softly sang "By the Light of the Silvery Moon," and then "Shine On, Harvest Moon."

Slowly, the night sky darkened as the lunar eclipse began.

Several minutes later . . .

Several minutes later, the last sliver of moonlight disappeared. The lunar eclipse was complete.

"There," said a proud Miss Scarlet sitting in the dark. "The moon is gone — and I'm still here."

She turned her head toward the door and called, "Mr. Boddy, you can untie me now!"

Hearing her voice, the guest with the Candlestick, not Mr. Boddy, entered the Study.

But Miss Scarlet was not there.

In another part of the mansion, the guest with

the Wrench tried to find Miss Scarlet in the Library.

Miss Scarlet was not there, either.

Not giving up, the guest tried the Billiard Room. No Miss Scarlet.

Thinking Miss Scarlet's voice came from the Kitchen, the guest with the Knife went there. But Miss Scarlet was not in the Kitchen, either.

The remaining guests ran into each other in the Hall.

"Have you found Miss Scarlet yet?" one asked.

"If I had, she would be eclipsed like the moon," the other said.

"Did you try the Conservatory?" the first guest asked.

"Yes," the other guest said. "She's not there."

"How about the Ball Room?"

"She's not there, either," the other guest said. "Nor in the Dining Room. Where is that woman?"

"Well, give me your weapon and I'll find her," the first guest said.

"Then leave me your weapon for protection," the second guest asked before handing over her weapon.

Armed with a new weapon, after another thorough search of the mansion, the first guest entered the remaining room and found Miss Scarlet helplessly tied to the chair.

"At last!" said Miss Scarlet. "Be a good friend and untie me, please."

"Not on your life. Maybe this will change your mind about silly superstitions," the guest said, raising the weapon and killing Miss Scarlet.

WHO MURDERED MISS SCARLET?
WHERE? AND WITH WHAT WEAPON?

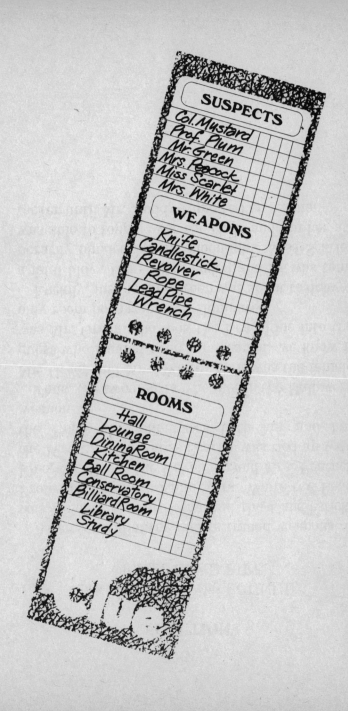

SOLUTION

MR. GREEN in the LOUNGE
with the LEAD PIPE

After several of the guests traded weapons, it was Colonel Mustard who had the Candlestick, Professor Plum the Knife, Mrs. White the Lead Pipe, Mr. Green the Revolver, and Mrs. Peacock the Wrench. Since Miss Scarlet was tied up with the Rope, this eliminates both her and her weapon.

Thus, the two guests who met in the Hall were Mr. Green and Mrs. White. As it was the female guest who handed over her weapon, we know it was Mr. Green who took the Lead Pipe into the only room not previously eliminated.

Luckily, just as Mr. Green was about to deliver a fatal blow, the eclipse ended and he was temporarily blinded by the moonlight. Miss Scarlet was able to topple over the chair and pin her attacker until Mr. Boddy came to her rescue.

8.
Doggone It!

IN GREAT DISTRESS, MR. BODDY called his guests into the Hall. There, he was holding his equally distressed French poodle named Oodle.

"*Yip, yip, yip!*" barked Oodle at the assembled guests.

"Oodle, hush," said Mr. Boddy.

But the dog was too upset to remain quiet. Oodle barked and growled at the guests.

"That dog should be sent to obedience school," suggested Mrs. Peacock.

"He's usually very well-behaved," said Mr. Boddy. "But something horrible has happened."

"What's wrong with Strudel?" asked Professor Plum.

"It's Oodle, you noodle!" hissed Mrs. White.

"Well, you don't have to bite his head off!" boomed Colonel Mustard. "I've challenged men to a duel for less than that."

"But, Colonel, your bark's always worse than your bite," said Mr. Green.

"Don't count on it!" Colonel Mustard growled back, showing his sharp white teeth.

Mr. Boddy interrupted the argument by saying, "Please, everyone, we're in the middle of a crisis."

"Don't tell me the stock market ticker isn't working!" said a worried Mr. Green.

"I hope you haven't canceled the etiquette lesson planned for tomorrow," said a very concerned Mrs. Peacock.

"Did one of my science experiments explode?" asked Professor Plum.

"I pray that the networks didn't substitute some silly presidential news conference for my favorite musical show, *Dueling Banjos*," said Colonel Mustard.

"Don't even think of telling me to expect a few more guests for dinner," said Mrs. White.

"No, no, no, no, no," said Mr. Boddy. "Oodle's been robbed!"

"Your dog has been robbed?" asked Mrs. Peacock.

"There have been reports of cat burglars," said Mr. Green, "but this is quite unusual."

"Perhaps," agreed Mr. Boddy, "but with all of you as my guests, anything can happen."

"What do you mean by that?" asked Colonel Mustard, prepared to defend his honor.

"Forgive me," said Mr. Boddy, "but it's been a dog of a day and my temper is short."

"What exactly happened?" asked Mrs. White.

"Five minutes ago," explained Mr. Boddy, "Oodle came running to me while I was reading my newspaper in the Dining Room. He was upset and barking."

"Maybe he was hungry," said Mrs. Peacock.

"Maybe he had a bone to pick with you," suggested Mr. Green.

"Maybe he needed to go outside," said Colonel Mustard.

"Maybe he wanted to play fetch," said Professor Plum.

"Maybe he wanted to make a mess of the mansion," complained Mrs. White.

"No," said Mr. Boddy. "He was upset because one of you stole his diamond dog collar right off his little furry neck!"

"How rude!" stormed Mrs. Peacock.

"I never!" said Mr. Green.

"Don't worry," said a calm Professor Plum. "We'll collie — I mean, collar — the thief!"

"If necessary, we'll call in the police and a German shepherd or two," added Colonel Mustard.

"Weren't you listening?" asked Professor Plum. "It's not Mr. Boddy's sheep, but his dog. A bunch of shepherds from whatever country won't be of much help — "

"Quiet!" warned Colonel Mustard, "I was referring to the K-9 corps, which can sniff out the culprit!"

"Will you please let Mr. Boddy finish his dastardly accusation?" asked Mrs. Peacock.

"I'm afraid it's true," said Mr. Boddy. "And

we're not leaving this room until we discover who committed such a clever canine crime."

"Maybe you should call in some of Oodle's friends to help solve this crime," suggested Mr. Green.

"Like?" asked Mr. Boddy.

"A pointer to point out the thief," Mr. Green said. "A retriever to retrieve the lost collar. A hound to hound the thief into confessing. A — "

"We get the idea," interrupted Mr. Boddy.

"Oodle's diamond collar is missing? Someone's in the doghouse, someone's in the doghouse," chanted Mrs. White.

"I'm afraid that you are a suspect as well, Mrs. White," reminded Mr. Boddy.

"Is this what I get for all my years of loyal service?" she asked. "And here I thought *I* was our man Boddy's best friend."

Mr. Green chuckled. "I'd be careful if I were you," he told Mrs. White. "If you see Mr. Boddy coming toward you with a rolled up newspaper in his hand, you should run the other way."

"*You'd* best be careful," Mrs. White shot back, "before someone yanks your chain."

"Heel!" Mr. Boddy told his guests.

"Well, I'm as innocent as a pup," said Professor Plum.

"Mrs. White, can you account for your whereabouts during the past hour since breakfast?"

76

asked Mr. Boddy. "That's when I last saw Oodle wearing his collar."

"I was doing the dishes," said Mrs. White. "I've only been in one room — the Kitchen."

"I was reading in the Library," said a male guest. "I saw neither hide nor hair of Strudel."

"Oodle, you noodle," said Mrs. White, again.

"I was in the Billiard Room," said Mr. Green, "and though I was playing billiards with a mutt, it wasn't Oodle."

"Do not call me a mutt or I shall challenge you to a duel!" cautioned a guest. "And besides, Mr. Green, I beat you soundly three games in a row. When it comes to billiards, *you* are the mutt."

"Well, at least we have an alibi," said Mr. Green.

"So do I," said a female guest. "I was helping Mrs. White do the dishes in the Kitchen."

"Is this true?" said a very surprised Mr. Boddy.

"Strange but true," answered Mrs. White. "Someone actually was helping me with the housework."

"How rude of you to even suspect me in the first place! I have the dishpan hands to prove it," said the guest, holding up her hands.

"That leaves you," said Mr. Boddy, turning to the remaining guest. "You haven't spoken a word since we gathered in the Hall. What do you have to say for yourself?"

"*Mummmmmanumanum*," said the guest, tight-lipped.

"What?" said Mr. Boddy.

"*Awummawumma!*"

"Cat got your tongue?" asked Mrs. White.

"*Ooorreemum*," muttered the guest.

"Some sort of dental problem?" asked Mr. Boddy.

"Like a problem with your canine tooth?" asked Mr. Green.

"I think we have our thief!" said Mrs. Peacock, turning to the guest. "Open your mouth!"

Reluctantly, the guest cooperated — revealing the stolen dog collar!

"A clever attempt," said Mr. Boddy. "But try to dog-paddle your way out of this one! Make no bones about it — you *are* in the doghouse."

WHO STOLE THE DIAMOND DOG COLLAR?

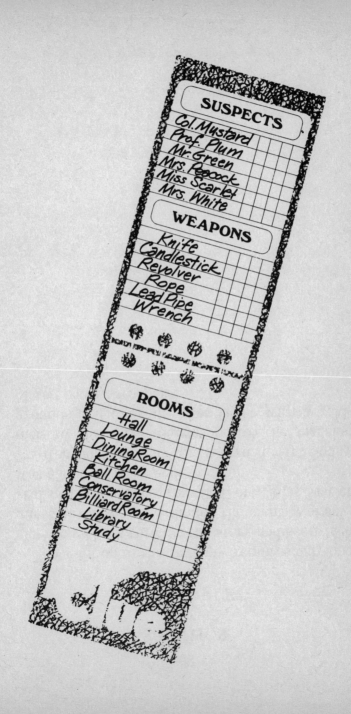

SOLUTION

MISS SCARLET

The solution to this mystery requires only one clue: to go back through the story and see which guest never spoke. Although the identity of several suspects was not revealed, only Miss Scarlet was silent until the end.

After Oodle's collar was returned, Mr. Boddy insisted that Miss Scarlet patrol the mansion grounds and clean up after Oodle with a gold-plated pooper-scooper.

9.
Sands of Time

Mr. BODDY CALLED HIS GUESTS INTO the Kitchen.

"Well, what's so important to take me from my reading?" asked Colonel Mustard.

"Colonel, don't tell me you were actually reading?" asked a surprised Mrs. Peacock.

"I was in the Library enjoying the latest edition of *Dueling for Dollars* magazine," Colonel Mustard replied. "Care to borrow it after I'm done? It has a lovely feature on sabers."

"No, thank you," said Mrs. Peacock. "I was busy in the Hall lining up Mr. Boddy's suits of armor in the proper posture. Luckily, I had the Lead Pipe to help me make a couple of adjustments."

Mr. Green looked around. "I don't see anything out of the ordinary, Mr. Boddy. Out with it, man!" he threatened with the Revolver.

"What could possibly be so important that you threaten our host with a gun?" asked Mrs. Peacock.

"He's taking me away from the stock market ticker in the Study," explained Mr. Green.

"And I was busy doing . . . doing . . . doing . . . well, something very, very important, I'm sure," added Professor Plum.

"Very well. I'll get a move on," said Mr. Boddy. He showed his guests a small hourglass half filled with sand.

"I know all too well what that is," said Mrs. White. "It's an egg timer."

"An egg timer?" yawned Miss Scarlet. "How exciting. And to think I rushed here from the Ball Room, where I was practicing ballet."

"I walked by the Ball Room and thought it was dark inside," commented Mrs. Peacock.

"It was meant to be dark. I was practicing *Sleeping Beauty*. It was dark, that is, except for the light coming from the Candlestick," said Miss Scarlet.

"Better be careful or you'll be dancing to *The Firebird*," warned Mrs. White.

"I'm always careful with the Candlestick," said Miss Scarlet. "It's the most romantic light for ballet."

"Well, I don't mind taking a break from my cleaning," sighed Mrs. White. "That Billiard Room is an awful mess. I had to knock the cobwebs down with this Rope."

"I've heard of a cowgirl using a lasso at a rodeo," said Mr. Green. "But a *cob*girl?"

"Come, come, Mr. Boddy," said Professor Plum. "What's so interesting about a silly egg timer? You interrupted my snack in the Dining Room." He held up an apple impaled on the Knife. "Anyone care for a slice?"

"How rude!" said Mrs. Peacock.

"I meant a slice of apple," said Professor Plum.

"Mr. Boddy, the secret of the egg timer remains with you alone," observed Colonel Mustard. "What is so unusual?"

"There's enough sand inside the glass to measure the passing of exactly three minutes," said Mr. Boddy. "The time needed to make the perfect soft-boiled egg."

"I think it's your brain that's soft-boiled," said Professor Plum. "And coming from me, that's not a flattering comment."

"What *is* this about?" stormed Colonel Mustard, waving the Wrench.

"Actually, this particular egg timer is very valuable," Mr. Boddy explained.

"Pray, tell," said Miss Scarlet.

"The sand inside is not ordinary sand," said Mr. Boddy. "It's actually grains of pure gold."

The guests were suddenly intrigued.

"I knew there was something I liked about that egg timer," said Miss Scarlet. She stood on the points of her ballet shoes for an extra-close look.

"The egg timer is one of the greatest inventions of all time," proclaimed Professor Plum. "It ranks right up there with the battery-powered toothbrush."

"It's certainly my favorite kitchen tool," said Mrs. White with a nod. "I can't imagine preparing breakfast — or any other meal, for that matter — without one."

"A device that measures three minutes and exactly three minutes every time, anywhere, no matter the weather," observed Mr. Green. "No wonder great fortunes have been made and lost over the marvelous thing we call by the simple words *egg timer*."

"If you'll give me that egg timer, I promise to complete my next duel in under three minutes," said Colonel Mustard.

"But I can recite the basic rules of proper manners in precisely three minutes," said Mrs. Peacock. "So the egg timer should go to me."

"I could use it to time my next experiment," said Professor Plum.

"Let me have the timer and for three minutes I'll stand on my toes without moving a muscle," promised Miss Scarlet.

"Give me three minutes and I'll make three million dollars on the bond market," boasted Mr. Green.

"I have a better idea," said Mr. Boddy. "In ten seconds, I'm going to turn the timer over and let the sand start to run out."

"And then?" asked Miss Scarlet.

"Each of you will have exactly three minutes to return to what you were doing," Mr. Boddy said.

He gestured to the intercom on the wall. "I'll be waiting there for each of you to check in," he added. "The first guest to do so will receive this priceless timer as a prize."

The guests lined up, elbowing one another to be closest to the door.

"The timer is mine!" said Mr. Green.

"I'm faster than you," boasted Mrs. White. "They don't call me 'Twinkle Toes' for nothing."

"But, thanks to ballet, my legs are stronger," said Miss Scarlet.

Mr. Boddy turned over the timer. The gold sand began to spill from the top half of the glass into the bottom half. He shouted, "Go!"

The guests rushed off.

That is, all but the guest with the Wrench, who attacked Mr. Boddy and stole the gold-filled timer.

The thief ran out of the Kitchen and into the Dining Room. There the thief tried to escape through the Dining Room window.

But the guest who was already there attacked him and stole the gold-filled timer. Holding the egg timer, the guest rushed toward the front door in the Hall.

There he was hit over the head with the Lead Pipe. He fell to the ground and lost the timer to his attacker.

The guest who now had the timer went into the Study and tried to hide it there. But seeing the guest with the Revolver in the room, the guest with the timer rushed out of the Study and through the Lounge. Unable to find a good place to hide the timer there, the guest next tried the Billiard Room.

There the guest with the timer was about to be lassoed by the guest with the Rope, but the thief scooted around the billiard table and rushed out of that room and into the Ball Room.

Picking up speed, the thief outran the guest with the Candlestick, executed a perfect ballet leap called a *jeté*, and raced out of the room.

Desperate, the guest with the timer fled to the only room not previously mentioned.

There, out of breath, the thief waited — until discovered by Mr. Boddy.

"How ever did you find me?" the thief asked.

"Your heavy breathing gave you away," said Mr. Boddy.

The thief watched the last gold grains fall from the top half of the egg timer into the bottom half. "Looks like I just ran out of time," the thief sighed.

"True," said Mr. Boddy. "But in the process, you set a new record in the hundred-meter dash."

WHO STOLE THE GOLD-FILLED TIMER?
WHERE WAS THE THIEF HIDING?

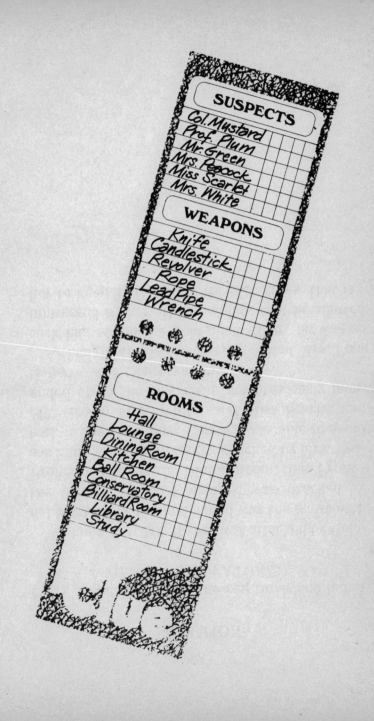

SOLUTION

MRS. PEACOCK stole the egg timer and hid in the CONSERVATORY.

We know that Mr. Boddy was attacked by Colonel Mustard because Mustard was the guest with the Wrench. Colonel Mustard was attacked by Professor Plum in the Dining Room, then Professor Plum was subsequently attacked by Mrs. Peacock in the Hall. Mrs. Peacock was able to avoid Mr. Green, Mrs. White, and Miss Scarlet and ended up in the only room not previously mentioned — the Conservatory.

Although Mr. Boddy was angry that Mrs. Peacock had stolen the gold-filled timer, he was so impressed by her athletic ability that he allowed her to keep it. For all of three minutes, that is.

10.
The Haunted Gargoyle

THE LAST NIGHT THAT THE GUESTS stayed at the mansion, Mr. Boddy called them into the Conservatory. The room was dark, except for a few candles.

"What's Mr. Boddy planning this time?" asked Mr. Green. "A conversation with the spirit world?"

"Would that be a long-distance call?" joked Mrs. White.

"It is kind of spooky in here," said Professor Plum, rubbing his arms for warmth.

"It's rude to frighten your guests," said Mrs. Peacock.

"Mrs. Peacock, a woman like you should like the dark," kidded Miss Scarlet. "It's hard to tell your age in this low light."

"It figures that I'd spend the whole afternoon cleaning this room and now no one can see it sparkle," said a tired Mrs. White.

"Mr. Boddy, I demand you shed some light on what's going on!" demanded Colonel Mustard.

"I want to create the proper atmosphere before

I show you my latest acquisition," explained Mr. Boddy.

"Let's see it," said Professor Plum. "As long as it's not too scary."

Mr. Boddy carefully unwrapped a small marble statue of a gargoyle. It had a monstrous face topped with horns. Wings sprouted from its shoulders. Tiny vampire teeth could be seen in its stony mouth.

"I take it that it's not supposed to look like you," said Mr. Green.

Mr. Boddy glared at him.

"Sorry," said Mr. Green.

"My goodness!" shouted a frightened Professor Plum. "It's the spitting image of the baby-sitter my parents left me with years ago when they went to Mexico!"

"No, no. This thing is hundreds of years old," said Mr. Boddy.

"So was the baby-sitter," said a shaken Professor Plum.

"Wherever did you find that ghastly thing?" asked Mrs. Peacock.

"One of my buyers found this curiosity in a small village in Transylvania," said Mr. Boddy.

"Transylvania?" asked Mr. Green. "Isn't that where vampires and werewolves come from?"

Mr. Boddy nodded. "The statue dates back to the fourteenth century and is very, very valuable."

"How valuable?" asked Colonel Mustard.

"The national museum has offered me five million dollars for it," said a proud Mr. Boddy.

"Why, that's the cutest thing," said Miss Scarlet.

"I loved my old baby-sitter," added Professor Plum.

"Who's afraid of a silly vampire or werewolf?" said Mr. Green with a shrug.

"I'll fight anyone for that gargoyle," added Colonel Mustard.

"That statue would make a proper addition to any home," said Mrs. Peacock. "Especially mine."

Secretly the guests all started plotting how to steal it.

"But I must warn you," added Mr. Boddy. "Legend has it that if this gargoyle falls into the wrong hands, strange things may happen."

"These are not the wrong hands," said Miss Scarlet. She showed hers, which were topped by ruby-red fingernails.

"Ridiculous!" protested Mr. Green.

"Legends are silly, made-up stories," said Colonel Mustard.

"I'm not afraid," said Mrs. Peacock.

"Please believe me," said Mr. Boddy.

"You mean that thing is truly haunted?" asked a worried Mrs. White.

"It can't be any worse than my baby-sitter," insisted Professor Plum.

"Steal it and find out," Mr. Boddy challenged his guests.

Later that night . . .

Later that night, Mr. Boddy and his guests went to bed early. They all had to be up early the next morning, since they were departing. With the guests packed and ready to go, the mansion appeared to be quiet.

Then a female guest crept into the room where Mr. Boddy had put the gargoyle and stole it.

She took the gargoyle into the Billiard Room, where she planned to hide it until she left the mansion in the morning.

"There's nothing haunted about this statue," the guest said to herself, using the Wrench to open a closet.

But while the guest's back was turned, the windows in the Billiard Room blew open without a warning. A strong gust pushed the guest into the closet, which mysteriously locked itself.

"Help! Help me!" Her muffled cries could be heard through the thick closet door.

Hearing the pleas, a male guest came downstairs and entered the room. He traced the noise to the closet.

"Is someone in there?" he asked.

"Yes! Open up! Please help me!"

"Hold on," he said.

He managed to open the closet by knocking the doorknob off with the Lead Pipe.

"Are you all right?" he asked the shaken guest inside the closet.

"I will be, once you help me out of here!" she said.

The male guest was about to extend a hand when he saw the gargoyle on the closet floor.

So instead of helping, he knocked out the original thief and stole the statue himself.

He took the gargoyle into the Lounge.

There, he flicked on the lights and examined the statue. "Legends are silly, made-up stories," he said to himself. "I'm not afraid."

Just then, the lights overhead went out.

"I'm afraid! I'm afraid!" the guest screamed.

The guest rushed from the room, glancing over his shoulder every few seconds.

He was about to enter the Library, but in his panic he was not looking where he was going. He ran smack into a wall and knocked himself out.

The statue rolled into the Library.

A third guest rushed downstairs. After a frantic search, the guest found the gargoyle on the Library floor.

"How did it get in here?" the guest wondered. "Maybe it *is* haunted!"

Being cautious, the guest used the Rope to collect the gargoyle.

"All this suspense has made me frightfully hungry," the guest said to herself.

The guest took the gargoyle into the Kitchen.

There she was surprised by another guest with the Revolver.

"Mrs. White, hand over the statue — or I'll shoot," the guest warned.

"First, Mr. Green, I must get something to eat!"

"Why are you so famished?" he asked.

"I don't know. Maybe the gargoyle put a spell on me," the other person said.

"Don't be silly! Hand that statue over this instant!" the guest with the Revolver insisted. "I'm going to sell it to the museum myself."

Having no choice, she handed over the gargoyle, and the guest with the Revolver fled into the Study.

The guest, pleased with himself, moved to the mirror above the mantel. "Let's see how I look with Mr. Boddy's prized statue," he said.

To the guest's horror, though, he stared at himself in the mirror and believed he was turning the same sickly color as his name.

"This thing *is* haunted," he moaned in a loud voice. "I have to get rid of it."

He rushed into the Ball Room, but the dark frightened him so much that he ran back into the Hall.

There, he was knocked out by another guest

with the Candlestick, who said, "Don't you know it's rude to be racing around the mansion? You'd think that you were being chased by ghosts!"

The guest with the Candlestick started up the stairs with the gargoyle. "I'll just slip this treasure in my suitcase and leave with it in the morning," she told herself.

"Haunted?" she added with a chuckle, reaching the top of the stairs. "Fiddlesticks! I'll teach this gargoyle some proper manners!"

But, an instant later, she tripped. Unable to regain her balance, she tumbled down the stairs and was knocked out.

In the process, the gargoyle landed on the soft rug in the Hall.

The remaining guest woke up.

"I was having the strangest dream about a haunted gargoyle," the guest said. "I'd best see if it was real or not."

The guest came downstairs and found the gargoyle statue on the floor.

"My, my," the guest said. "Here's my chance to steal it."

The guest happily took the gargoyle into the remaining room.

Mr. Boddy woke, too. "It's awfully quiet," he said. "Too quiet, if you ask me."

Sensing something was terribly wrong, he pulled on a robe and rushed downstairs.

He stepped over the fallen guest lying at the

base of the stairs and began to search the mansion.

Mr. Boddy went from room to room until at last he found the thief.

"Give me back my statue before it's too late," Mr. Boddy warned. "The gargoyle is haunted!"

"It's harmless," the guest replied, "but I'm not!"

With that, the guest murdered Mr. Boddy.

WHO KILLED MR. BODDY?
IN WHICH ROOM?
WITH WHAT WEAPON?

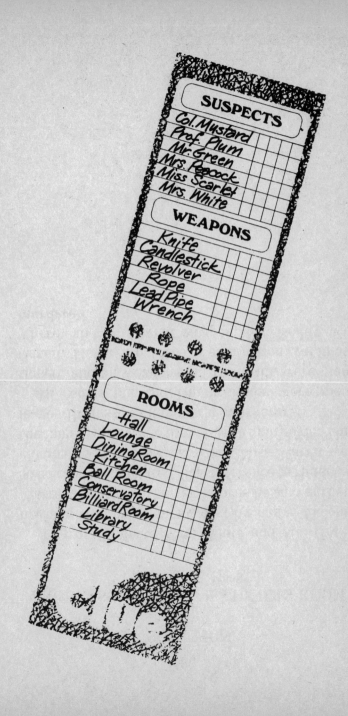

SOLUTION

PROFESSOR PLUM in the DINING ROOM with the KNIFE

We can eliminate Mrs. White and Mr. Green because they were mentioned by name. Colonel Mustard repeated the very words he said earlier, so he can be eliminated. The reference to rudeness eliminates Mrs. Peacock. Thus, Miss Scarlet was the female guest who first stole the gargoyle. This leaves Professor Plum as the murderer.

All rooms but the Dining Room were mentioned, and all weapons but the Knife were mentioned. Through process of elimination, we know where, and with what weapon, Mr. Boddy was murdered.